Mrs. Wishy-Washy
and the Big Tub

HAMERAY
PUBLISHING GROUP

Mrs. Wishy-Washy took her animals to the Sunshine train.

"Four tickets to the sea," she said to the ticket man.

3

"Okay," the ticket man replied.
"But no feet on seats!"

"You will have to stand,"
Mrs. Wishy-Washy said to her animals.

4

Clicketty-clack! Clicketty-clack!
At last, the Sunshine train stopped
at Sunshine Beach.

Mrs. Wishy-Washy pointed to the water.
"The sea is like a big tub!" she said.

The animals had never seen
such a big tub of water.
Moo moo! Oink oink!
Quack, quack, quack!

Splash!

They jumped in the waves.

They swam and splashed each other.

This big tub was fun.

Afterward, they played in the sand.
Sand in feathers! Sand in hair!
Sand in snout! Sand everywhere!

"Have a sandwich,"
said Mrs. Wishy-Washy.

It was time to go home
on the Sunshine train.
"Four tickets to home,"
said Mrs. Wishy-Washy.

"Okay," said the ticket man.
"But remember! No feet on seats!"

"No feet on seats,"
said Mrs. Wishy-Washy.